Some words about coconuts:

"Spin me faster! Spin me faster!
Spin me faster!"
Daisy
☆
"Win me! Win me! Win me!"
Dolphin key ring
☆
"Eat me! Eat me! Eat Me!"
Stick of candyfloss
☆
**"Activating
invisible force fields
NOW!"**
Coconut-shy man
☆
"I'm going to be sick!"
Stephanie Brakespeare

D0270376

More Daisy adventures!

DAISY AND THE TROUBLE
WITH LIFE

DAISY AND THE TROUBLE
WITH ZOOS

DAISY AND THE TROUBLE
WITH GIANTS

DAISY AND THE TROUBLE
WITH KITTENS

DAISY AND THE TROUBLE
WITH CHRISTMAS

DAISY AND THE TROUBLE
WITH MAGGOTS

DAISY

and the TROUBLE with

COCONUTS

by Kes Gray

RED FOX

DAISY AND THE TROUBLE WITH COCONUTS
A RED FOX BOOK 978 1 849 41678 8

First published in Great Britain by Red Fox,
an imprint of Random House Children's Publishers UK
A Random House Group Company

This edition published 2012

3 5 7 9 10 8 6 4 2

The Random House Group Limited supports the Forest Stewardship Council
(FSC®), the leading international forest certification organization. Our books
carrying the FSC label are printed on FSC®-certified paper. FSC is the only forest
certification scheme endorsed by the leading environmental organizations,
including Greenpeace. Our paper procurement policy can be found
at www.randomhouse.co.uk/environment.

MIX
Paper from
responsible sources
FSC® C016897

Set in Vag Rounded 15 / 23pt

RANDOM HOUSE CHILDREN'S PUBLISHERS UK
61–63 Uxbridge Road, London W5 5SA

www.randomhousechildrens.co.uk
www.totallyrandombooks.co.uk
www.randomhouse.co.uk

Addresses for companies within The Random House Group Limited can be found at:
www.randomhouse.co.uk/offices.htm

THE RANDOM HOUSE GROUP Limited Reg. No. 954009

A CIP catalogue record for this book is available from the British Library.

Printed and bound in Great Britain by CPI Group (UK) Ltd, Croydon, CR0 4YY

To Oliver Edward Andrews

CHAPTER 1

The **trouble with coconuts** is they are the worst type of nuts in the whole wide world.

If I was a monkey living in a jungle that was totally made up of coconut trees, and one of the coconuts on one of the trees asked me to be their friend, then there is absolutely no way that I would say yes. I'd rather be friends with Jack Beechwhistle, who's the worst boy on earth, than be friends with a coconut.

If you ask me, coconuts shouldn't be allowed in a funfair. If you double ask me, they shouldn't even be allowed to grow. Coconuts are too big. Coconuts are too hairy. Plus, if you try to win one, they just get you into trouble.

WHICH ISN'T MY FAULT!

CHAPTER 2

I was really excited when I heard that the funfair was coming to town. Gabby was the first person at school to tell me. Nishta Bagwhat was second. Daniel McNicholl was third.

Fiona Tucker was fourth, I think. Or it might have been Colin Kettle, I'm not sure. So I'll call it a draw.

Everyone in the playground was really excited about the funfair. Trouble is, everyone was still really excited when we went into class too. Being excited about funfairs in class is against school rules. Because it makes you forget your times tables. And it makes you fidget.

The **trouble with fidgeting** is it makes your chair squeak.

The **trouble with chairs squeaking** is it makes your teacher look right at you. Which is a bit of a problem if you've just said six sevens are 93.

If you've just told your teacher that six sevens are 93, you really want her to ask someone else the next sum.

Trouble is, when Mrs Peters heard my chair squeak again, she asked me two sums in a row. Which is probably against the law. But there was no one around to stop her.

The **trouble with nine times eight** is it's an even harder sum to do than six times seven. Especially if there's a funfair coming to town.

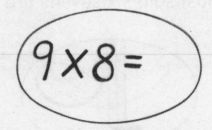

If there's a funfair coming to town, all sums turn into really hard sums because your brain can't stop thinking about more important things.

Like funfairs.

The **trouble with thinking about funfairs during mental arithmetic** is the nines sound a bit like fives and the eights get muddled up with fours.

Which is why I said that the answer to nine times eight was 20.

Which isn't the right answer either.

When Mrs Peters said it wasn't even close, everyone in my class started looking at me. Which made me go all hot.

The **trouble with going all hot in class** is it makes your brain shrink. Which means it's even harder to do sums in your head.

Luckily for me, Jack Beechwhistle fell off his chair just before I was going to change my mind to 76. Which was a good job really. Because 76 wasn't the right answer either.

Thank goodness Jack *did* fall off his chair, because everyone was

looking at him now, instead of me.
Including Mrs Peters.

Except no one could see him.
Because he hadn't got back up off
the floor.

When Fiona Tucker looked down

by her feet and told us that Jack was dead on the floor, Mrs Peters forgot about nine times eight altogether. She ran to the back of the class where Fiona and Jack sit and looked under the desk to see if it was true.

But it wasn't. Jack Beechwhistle wasn't even slightly dead. He was just pretending.

That's the **trouble with Jack Beechwhistle**. He is soooooooooooo badly behaved.

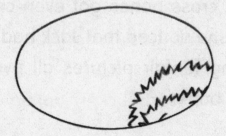

The **trouble with pretending you're dead in class** is Mrs Peters doesn't think it's a very funny thing to do.

Everyone else in class thought it was funny, but Mrs Peters is a teacher. Which means she's had her funny bones taken out and replaced with cross bones.

Her cross bones got even crosser when she noticed that Jack had been drawing funfair pictures all over his maths book.

Then she got even crosser than crosser when she noticed that Fiona Tucker had been drawing funfair pictures too.

$$4 \times 10 = 40$$
$$2 \times 8 = 16$$
$$6 \times 7 =$$

It wasn't just Jack and Fiona either.

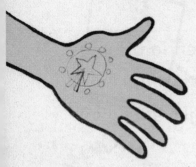

Nishta had drawn a big wheel on the back of her hand, Harry Bayliss had done a candyfloss

tattoo on his arm and David Alexander had drawn a rifle

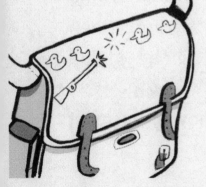

range with exploding ducks right across the top of his school bag.

No wonder no one could get their sums right.

Luckily I'd never been to a funfair before, so I didn't know what kind of pictures to draw. But I still got told off for squeaking.

Mrs Peters told us that fidgeting and drawing funfair pictures in mental arithmetic was completely unacceptable behaviour. She said that if Pythagoras had spent all his time fidgeting and drawing candyfloss tattoos on his arms, then mathematics would still be in the Dark Ages.

She said that from now on we must

start concentrating on the important things in life. Then she said we had to stay in at break time to catch up on our sums. Plus we got banned from even thinking about funfairs for the rest of the day.

But I still did. Only in secret and without fidgeting!

CHAPTER 3

The **trouble with funfair posters** is when a funfair comes to town, they stick them everywhere!

When me and Mum went into town after school, I saw funfair posters stuck on the fence down by the roundabout. There were funfair posters stuck on the window of an empty shop in the high street. There were even bits of a funfair poster stuck on the back of a lorry parked outside the baker's.

It was so exciting!

It got even more exciting when Mum told me that Nanny and Grampy had phoned while I was at school and offered to take me to the funfair on Saturday afternoon! I didn't even know that my nanny and grampy liked funfairs! I thought they were far too old to like fun things.

Mum said that just because people are over the age of sixty it doesn't mean they should give up the will to live. She said that, for a lot of people, retirement is the most enjoyable time of life. She said that when you're Nanny and Grampy's age you can do anything you want, any time you want to.

Which is a good job really, because Mum would never have taken me to a funfair. Because Mum doesn't like funfairs at all.

Whenever the funfair has come to town before, my mum has always pulled a grumpy face. As far as she is concerned, funfairs are a complete waste of money. Plus she says the games at a funfair are too expensive and the rides spin you round so much they make you sick.

Sometimes I think my mum should have been a teacher.

Luckily for me, Mum wasn't invited. I reckon Nanny and Grampy had probably taken Mum to a funfair when she was a little girl and had decided never to do it again. Funfairs are no fun at all if you take the wrong sort of children.

Luckily for Nanny and Grampy, I was exactly the right sort of child to take to a funfair. I didn't mind if the rides were too expensive because Nanny and Grampy would be paying! I didn't even mind if the rides made me feel sick, because at least I'd be having brilliant fun at the same time! Plus I was absolutely sure I wasn't going to be sick anyway.

When I spoke to Grampy on the phone on Friday, he sounded even more excited about the funfair than me! He asked me if I'd ever been in a bumper car, and I said I hadn't. He asked me if I'd ever been down a helter-skelter, and I said I hadn't. He asked me if I'd ever been on a waltzer, and I said I hadn't. He asked me if I'd ever eaten a toffee apple, and I said I had.

But I hadn't. Only I said I had because it was getting a bit embarrassing. And anyway, I HAD eaten an apple before. And I HAD eaten a toffee before. Only not at the same time. Which is almost the same thing.

Kind of.

Anyway, Grampy said that there were two things that we absolutely *must* do while we were at the funfair on Saturday.

Number 1: We *must* win a goldfish!

Number 2: We *must* win a coconut!

I'd never won a goldfish or a coconut before, so you can imagine how excited I was now!!

When Nanny came on the phone, she said that they would pick me up in the car at twelve o'clock on Saturday and would bring me back at four.

Which, if you're any good at mental arithmetic, adds up to . . .

. . . **FOUR** FABULOUS FUN-FILLED HOURS!

Maybe staying in at break time *did* help me with my sums after all!

CHAPTER 4

The **trouble with normal breakfasts** is they can be a bit boring.

So when I woke up on Saturday I decided that instead of having a normal breakfast, I would have a special funfair one. Funfair breakfasts are much more fun. In fact they're so much fun, you don't even need to put sugar on them!

To have a funfair breakfast, all you need is two Weetabixes and some Honey Nut Loops. Oh, and a biggish carton of milk with quite a lottish amount of milk in.

Here are my instructions on how to make Daisy's Special Funfair Breakfast:

First of all, take the first Weetabix and lay it flat on the bottom of your bowl.

Then wedge the second Weetabix up against it like a slide. (The first Weetabix helps the second Weetabix stay in position.)

Next, cover the flat Weetabix with milk. Not too much – just enough to make the milk look like a swamp.

Then, take a Honey Nut Loop in your fingers, place it at the top of the slide, count down from three to one, let go of the Honey Nut Loop and let it roll down the slide into the swamp!

As soon as the loop touches the side of your bowl, you can grab it out with your fingers and eat it!

How much fun is that?!

The more Honey Nut Loops you roll down the slide, the more you get to eat!! It's simple! Plus, once you've run out of Honey Nut Loops you can eat the slide while it's still crunchy and the mushy bottom of the swamp afterwards!!

Mum said I could have funfair breakfasts every day if it meant I was going to eat that much breakfast for breakfast.

I said I would if I could go to a funfair every day too.

But she said I couldn't.

So I said I probably wouldn't.

CHAPTER 5

It was a really hot day on Saturday, so getting dressed after breakfast took hardly any time at all. I was sure the funfair would be full of bright colours

so I decided to wear my brand-new orange shorts plus my brightest coloured T-shirt and socks.

Mum said I looked a bit clashy, but I didn't care. I think orange, purple and green go really well together.

Once I was dressed, I went into the lounge to practise my screaming. Gabby had told me that some of the rides at a funfair are so good, you can't stop screaming from the moment you get on!

The **trouble with practising screaming** is I'm too good at it.

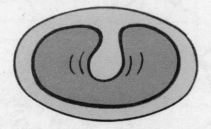

Mum said that if I wanted to practise my screaming I should go and do it outside in the garden.

But after about five screams our neighbour Mrs Pike told me that I should practise in the shed.

With the door shut.

So I did.

Except Tiptoes was asleep in the wheelbarrow.

The **trouble with screaming when Tiptoes is asleep in the wheelbarrow** is it doesn't just wake him up, it makes him go totally loopy.

I mean, one minute he was curled up in the wheelbarrow; the next minute he was halfway up the wall, then the other wall and then almost across the ceiling!

I wouldn't have screamed if I'd known he was there, but it was so dark in the shed there was no way I could see a cat curled up in the shadows.

That's the **trouble with cats**. If they wore fluorescent pyjamas when they went to sleep, they'd be much easier to see.

By the time I'd opened the shed door to let Tiptoes out, he'd knocked over the flower pots, the rake, the watering can, the spade, the fork, plus all the seed packets that were on the highest-up shelf.

And guess who had to pick them all up? It wasn't Tiptoes. It was me!

If you ask me, if a cat wants to curl up and go to sleep in a wheelbarrow he should get his own shed to sleep in. And his own wheelbarrow.

Or at least wear glow-in-the-dark pyjamas.

Or learn to snore loudly.

It was only when I was stretching

up high to put the seed packets back that I suddenly forgave Tiptoes for everything. Because all of my really high up stretching and stretching suddenly reminded me of something really important that Dylan had told me at school!

If you're going to go to a funfair . . .

. . . you need to wear your highest shoes!

CHAPTER 6

Dylan is the coolest boy I know. He's two years older than me, which means he's really experienced. Plus he lives two doors away from me in a house with a three-chime doorbell. AND he's got a pet snake called Shooter. How cool is that?

At first, when Dylan told me that I needed to wear my highest shoes to the funfair on Saturday, I thought he was joking. But Dylan is far too cool to do jokes. Sometimes Dylan is too cool to even smile.

According to Dylan, some of the rides at a funfair are so dangerous and so death-defying, you have to be over 140 centimetres to go on them! Trouble is, I'm only 134 centimetres tall.

The **trouble with being 134 centimetres tall** is that if you want to go on all the rides, you need to find an extra six centimetres from somewhere.

Trouble is, I didn't really know where to look.

When I asked my mum on Saturday morning what I needed to eat if I wanted to grow six centimetres in two hours, she wasn't very helpful at all.

"You could try eating some giraffe burgers," she laughed.

I don't know why she was laughing because it wasn't a very funny thing to say at all. Plus I couldn't try eating giraffe burgers because we don't have any giraffe burgers in our freezer.

We don't even have any cow burgers in our freezer any more, because my new super-health-conscious mum has suddenly decided that things that taste really nice like burgers aren't very good for me.

Or chicken nuggets.

According to my mum, it's time I started putting some healthier things inside me. Like fish without breadcrumbs and broccoli without tomato sauce.

Mum watches far too much telly, if you ask me. Plus she's useless at helping to find extra centimetres.

The **trouble with putting on your mum's high heels** is if she sees you, she'll make you take them straight off.

The **trouble with wearing two pairs of shoes at once** is the first pair keep falling off.

The **trouble with sellotaping books to the bottom of your shoes** is the sellotape unsticks after about six steps, plus if the books belong to your mum, she gets a bit cross.

Especially if she hasn't read them yet.

Which means you STILL need to find another six centimetres from somewhere.

In the end my mum convinced me I didn't need to find six centimetres from anywhere. She said I wasn't going to a theme park where the rides are massive, I was going to a travelling funfair where the rides would be much smaller and not that death-defying at all.

Which was a bit disappointing really, because I wanted all the rides at the funfair to be as deathly death-defying as possible.

Mum said if I wanted to do something deathly death-defying, then I should try tidying my bedroom. Which wasn't funny either.

Then she said that there would be more than enough rides for me to go on at the funfair, more than enough rides for Nanny and Grampy to waste their money on, and more than enough rides to make me feel sick.

Which meant that 134 centimetres would be ample.

And actually, she was right.

For once.

She isn't usually right about anything. She's usually always wrong.

But I still put three pairs of socks on just in case!

CHAPTER 7

When Nanny and Grampy arrived outside our house in their car, I nearly screamed I was so excited!

"Are you ready to win a goldfish, Daisy?" shouted Grampy as he opened the door of his car.

"I sure am!" I shouted back.

"Are you ready to win a coconut?" he shouted as he opened the garden gate for Nanny.

"You bet!" I shouted back.

If I could have, I would have run straight out of the front door, raced

49

down the garden path and jumped straight into their car through the sunroof, I was so excited!

Trouble is, Mum made me put some sun cream on first.

The **trouble with putting on sun cream** is it takes ages. Especially if it's a hot day, because more of your burny bits are on show.

Which meant Nanny and Grampy had to come into our house and wait for me.

Which meant Mum had a chance to talk to them about some really boring stuff like:

"Don't let Daisy get over over-excited," and "Don't let Daisy go on rides that will make her sick."

Honestly, sometimes I wonder if Mum was ever an actual child herself.

If she was, I bet she never got sunburned.

Mum made me put so much sun cream on, it was twenty past twelve before we even left the house!

Grampy said I looked like a polar bear when I got in the car.

That's the **trouble with sun cream for children**. Children don't want to put it on in the first place, plus when you're made to, it's all white and smeary.

The **trouble with short-sleeved T-shirts** is the sleeves are too short to wipe your face on.

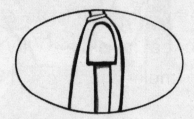

The **trouble with wiping your face on your arms** is if your arms are white and smeary too, then the white from your face will smear onto your arms and the white from your arms will smear onto your face.

Which means that, after loads of wiping, you still look like a polar bear!

I mean, why can't sun cream for children be invisible? Why does it have to make them look like polar bears?

I mean, grown-up sun cream isn't thick and white and smeary, is it? Sun cream for grown-ups is invisible. Which means it just makes grown-ups look like grown-ups. Only slimier.

That's definitely something I'm going to invent when I'm older. Invisible non-smeary sun cream for children.

And extra-thick extra-white extra-smeary sun cream for grown-ups. So *they* can look like polar bears instead. Which will serve them right.

Luckily Nanny had some tissues in her handbag. Otherwise I don't know what I'd have done.

Nanny had mints in her handbag too! Which made me feel even better.

The **trouble with mints** is they're really hard to suck. Especially when you're driving to a funfair.

The **trouble with driving to a funfair** is it makes your teeth get excited.

The **trouble with excited teeth** is it's almost impossible to stop them from biting. Which is a bit of a problem really if your grampy suddenly says, "I know. Let's all play a game! Let's see who can suck a mint for the longest without crunching!"

At first I thought it was a really good idea for a game to play in the car. In fact, at first I did some really good sucks.

Then I saw the funfair poster down by the roundabout.

The **trouble with seeing a funfair poster** is your gums get excited too.

Then I counted three more funfair posters in the high street.

Which meant my tongue got excited.

Then I saw someone carrying a balloon that I was absolutely sure must have come from the funfair.

Which made my taste buds get excited.

And then, as we got nearer and nearer to the park, I actually heard actual funfair sounds coming through the actual sunroof of our actual car!

When I wound down my window, the sounds got even louder.

Which meant my everything buds got excited.

By the time we got to the car park and I got to actually *see* the funfair with my own eyes, even my dribble was excited!!!!!!!!!!

Which meant I had to crunch.

Which meant I lost the game.

Plus I bit my tongue.

Which hurt a bit. But it was OK.

Because for the first time ever in my life, it was

FUNFAIR, HERE I COME!

CHAPTER 8

The **trouble with seeing an actual funfair right in front of you** is you don't know where to look first!!!

It was so bright and colourful and noisy and busy! There were coloured lights and loud screaming sounds, there were big stripy tents held up by big thick ropes.

Plus there were people and children everywhere. It was as though everyone in the whole wide world had come to have fun at the funfair. Except my mum.

And guess what?

You didn't even have to pay to get in! All we had to do was park our car in the field, walk across the grass and go straight inside!

I didn't even have to be measured to see how high I was!

It was so brilliant! And so confusing! My left leg wanted to go left, my right leg wanted to go right, and my head – well, my head just wanted to go everywhere.

Before I'd had time to even think about goldfish or coconuts, I ran straight over to a stall with a green and yellow stripy roof and a big red sign with gold letters that said TOMBOLA!

Tombola is a really exciting funfair game. Once you have paid a lady some money you get to pick three chopped-up straws out of a bucket of sawdust. All the straws have rolled-up raffle tickets inside them, and if one of the raffle tickets has a number that ends in zero, you win a prize!

I was really good at pulling the rolled-up raffle tickets out of my straws, and even better at getting them to uncurl.

Trouble is, the raffle tickets I picked out of the bucket ended in 3, 6 and 9.

Which means I didn't win a prize. But it was OK, because there were loads of other stalls with flashing lights and stripy roofs to choose from.

The next game I tried was called hook-a-duck.

The **trouble with hook-a-duck** is you really need to be an expert fisherman to be good at it. Which is a shame for other children, because they haven't been taught to fish by my uncle Clive. Luckily I have.

Hook-a-duck is one of the most skilful funfair games you can ever play. Once you have paid a man some money, he gives you a stick with a string and a magnet dangling from it. That's your hook-a-duck fishing rod.

But then it gets even harder!

Not only have you got to learn how to dangle the string and the magnet from the end of your rod; you have to lean over a great big tank full of actual water at the same time!

And then it gets even harder!

Because the tank of water is where all the ducks are floating!!!

(Not actual ducks. Yellow plastic ones. With magnets on their backs.)

And then it gets even harder!

Because what you have to do then is use your hook-a-duck fishing rod to try and hook a duck out of the water!

The **trouble with a hook-a-duck duck** is it can only get hooked out if you can get the magnet at the end of your string to stick to the magnet on its back!

Which means you need to be a total fishing expert.

Which I am. So I did! In about seven seconds flat!

When I lifted my hook-a-duck duck out of the water I thought I was going to be able to keep it as a prize. But the hook-a-duck man turned my h o o k - a - d u c k duck upside down and showed me a black cross that had been felt-tipped onto its tummy.

A black cross means you can't keep the duck. And you haven't won a prize either. Which was a bit of a shame, but it didn't really matter

because I had already seen the next game I wanted to play!

It was in a tent about ten kangaroo jumps away and it was a game I'd always, always wanted to play . . . actual DARTS!

To play actual darts you have to pay a lady some money and then she gives you three actual darts! The actual darts she gave me looked just like the ones you see on telly, only a bit fatter, with yellow plastic bits on the end. At first I thought the sharp bits might have been dipped in poison, but Nanny said you aren't allowed to have poison darts at a funfair.

The **trouble with actual darts** is it's a lot harder to play than it looks. Especially if you're only 134 centimetres tall.

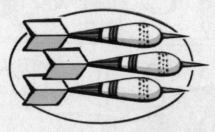

To win a prize at actual darts you have to throw all three darts at the dartboard and score less than 21. Which sounds easy, but is actually really hard.

When I went up to throw my first dart, I could hardly see the dartboard, which meant when I let go of the dart it kind of didn't go in the dartboard at all. It went in the lady's shoulder.

Luckily it didn't have poison on it and it didn't stick in very far. Otherwise

she wouldn't have let me have that go again. But she probably still would have got me a box to stand on.

When you're playing actual darts and you've got a box to stand on, the dartboard is much easier to see. Trouble is, it doesn't make it much easier to hit.

The **trouble with fat darts with yellow bits** is that when you throw them they never go straight.

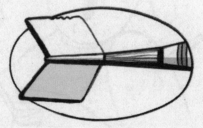

Plus, even when they hit the dartboard, they don't stick in.

My first dart nearly hit the dartboard. My second dart nearly hit the dartboard. My third dart DEFINITELY hit the dartboard, but it still ended up on the ground.

Which, if you add up all the scores, is zero. Which is definitely less than 21.

When I asked the lady for my prize, she told me that if the dart doesn't stick in the dartboard it counts as 1000. Which meant I'd scored 3000. Which is slightly more than 21.

When I asked if I could have

another go, Nanny and Grampy said we should probably move on. So did the lady.

Which was a good idea actually, because now I was about to go on my first ride!

CHAPTER 9

When I saw the bumper cars, I nearly wet myself! Bumper cars are totally the best! Not only has the bumper-car track got hundreds of flashing lights and really loud music, it's got cars you can actually drive!

And crash!

On purpose!!!!!!

Grampy said he loved going on bumper cars when he was a boy and he would come in my bumper car with me.

I said I definitely, definitely wanted

to be the driver!

Trouble is, you can't just get in and drive a bumper car straight away. You have to wait around the edge until all the people in the cars finish their go first.

When the hooter went and the bumper cars started to slow down, I had already worked out which one I wanted to drive. It was a bright shiny red one with a big grey rubber bumping bit round it. Plus it had my lucky number 8 on both sides!

As soon as the cars came to a proper stop I raced straight across to car number 8 and waited for the boy inside it to get out. Trouble is, he was a bit slow undoing his seat belt.

The **trouble with boys who are slow at undoing seat belts** is it makes you really impatient with them.

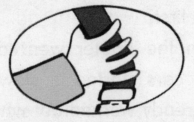

The **trouble with trying to undo their seat belt for them** is they don't really like it. Especially if they're about fifteen.

When I grabbed the boy's seat-belt buckle, he got really huffy and pushed my hand away. I think he was nearly going to say something not very nice to me, but then he saw that Grampy wanted to get into the bumper car with me, so he didn't say anything at all.

But even if he had I wouldn't have cared, because now I was sitting behind the wheel of my very own bumper car!

When I squeezed my fingers around my bumper car steering wheel, I got racing car tingles right through my body.

When Grampy fastened my seat belt, I felt like a grand-prix driver off the telly!

At first we started off quite slowly, but after about ten seconds I was driving our bumper car at full speed!

If I turned the steering wheel to the left, we went to the left! If I turned the wheel to the right, we went to the right. And if a car stopped in front of me, I could press my speed pedal as hard as I could and crash right into the back of them! Without saying sorry!

It was bumptastic!!!

Grampy asked me if I'd been taking driving lessons from my mum.

Then he told me to wave to Nanny.

The **trouble with waving to Nanny** is if you're driving a bumper car at the same time, you might miss someone you should be crashing into.

Luckily Grampy grabbed the steering wheel and made sure we bumped straight into car number 22!

And then car number 7, car number 12 and car number 9!

Grampy said we should try and crash into every single car before the hooter went! Trouble is, then the bumper-car man jumped onto the back of our car and told us we weren't allowed to bump.

Apparently we weren't in a bumper car, we were in a dodgem

car. Which meant bumping wasn't allowed. We had to dodge instead.

The **trouble with dodging cars instead of bumping them** is it's still really good fun but crashing into people is much better.

Grampy said it was health and safety gone mad, so we kept on doing it and doing it and doing it! Until I hit my chin on the steering wheel.

Which wasn't my fault. It was car number 14's fault.

The **trouble with car number 14** is I don't think the driver can have heard the hooter.

After the hooter goes you're not meant to bump anyone any more.

So when car number 14 suddenly crashed into me from behind, I couldn't stop myself from crashing forward and hitting my chin. Because I wasn't expecting to be bumped.

Luckily it wasn't my nose, because that really would have hurt! It still made me feel a little bit dizzy though.

Grampy said that if you bump someone in a dodgem car, it makes them want to bump you back. Even after the hooter has hooted.

Grampy undid my seat belt, had a good look at my chin, gave it a rub and said that these things happen, especially when there are maniac drivers around.

Which makes you think, doesn't it?

Why, oh, why don't bumper cars have airbags?

CHAPTER 10

The **trouble with being in a car accident** is it makes you need a fizzy drink.

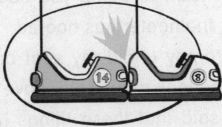

The **trouble with fizzy drinks** is there are so many different ones to choose from.

And non-fizzy ones! Especially at a funfair!

By the time I got to the fizzy drinks stall, I'd forgotten all about the bump on my chin. Fizzy drinks stalls give children much more important things to think about. Like cola, or cherryade, or lemonade or orangeade or, even better . . . wait for it . . .

. . . SLUSH PUPPIES!

When I saw that the fizzy drinks stall did slush puppies, I really did scream! Slush puppies are my favouritest drink that I'm not allowed to have. They're like milkshakes except they take all the milk out and put icy slush in instead. My mum never lets me have slush puppies because she says they're full of colourings and artificial flavourings and other things that sound really nice.

But guess what? My mum wasn't with us!

There are four flavours of slush puppy that you can choose from at a funfair. Green, red, orange and bright blue. Nanny and Grampy said I could have any flavour I wanted.

So after they had given the lady some money, I asked for red.

Mixed with bright blue.

Which makes bright purple if you

mix it up with a straw.

Bright purple slush puppies are the best! You should try one!

After I'd finished my slush puppy, Nanny said we should think about getting something to eat. Which was a brilliant idea, because my slush puppy had made me feel really hungry.

The **trouble with funfair hotdogs and burgers** is it's really hard to choose which one is nicest. Especially when the burgers are extra large and the sausages are extra long and bendy.

So Nanny said I could have one of each! So I did!

Without onions though.

The **trouble with funfair onions** is they look a bit burned and squishy.

Plus if you don't have any, it leaves much more room for tomato sauce.

After I'd eaten my hotdog and burger I thought I was absolutely full. But then I suddenly realized I wasn't! Because guess what I saw next?

CANDYFLOSS!

The **trouble with candyfloss** is when you see somewhere that makes it, it makes you do two things:

1. Scream.
2. Scream again!!

Have you ever seen how candy-floss is made? It's incredible! You just give a man some money and then he takes an empty stick and waves it round and round like a magic wand

inside this special metal machine where all the candyfloss is being fluffed up. The more waving he does, the more the candyfloss fluffs up onto your stick!

Nanny and Grampy asked the candyfloss man for an extra-large one, which meant by the time he had stopped fluffing, the candyfloss on my stick was huge!

In fact, it was bigger than my face!

Luckily I'm quite strong so I could hold it in one hand.

When I took my first bite of candyfloss, I couldn't believe it. It was like eating a pink sugary cloud! It tasted really sweet and really good for me, except every time I tried to chew it, it just melted away in my mouth! Big chews, little chews, tiny nibbles, weeny sucks – whichever way I tried to eat it, it just kept disappearing in my mouth.

Even if I just touched it with my tongue, it melted away!

After about twenty bites, Nanny showed me how to pull bits off with my fingers. If you pull candyfloss off with your fingers, it doesn't melt away at all. Until you put it in your mouth.

Then Nanny showed me how to use my candyfloss to pretend I had a moustache like Grampy's!

Only mine was a moustache I could eat!

"I've got a good idea!" I said. "I'll make a long candyfloss beard as well and pretend I'm Father Christmas!"

Trouble is, I didn't have enough candyfloss left on my stick by then. I only had about enough for a smallish mouse beard.

Which was OK, because now we were going on the waltzer!

CHAPTER 11

The **trouble with waltzers** is everybody wants to go on them. Which means we had to queue up in a line for about five minutes before we could get on.

Grampy said the queue would give my slush puppy and hotdog and burger and tomato sauce and candyfloss a chance to go down. But it also gave me a chance to say hello to Sanjay Lapore!

At first I didn't even realize that Sanjay and his mum and dad were standing in the queue behind us! I was far too busy watching the waltzer, trying to work out which carriage would be the fastest one for us to get into.

Sanjay asked me if I'd seen any friends from school. He said loads of people from school were at the funfair too – he had seen Liam Chaldecott, Liberty Pearce, Barry Morely, Vicky Carrow, Paula Potts and even Mrs Peters!

Can you believe it?! Mrs Peters!!!! I never thought she would like funfairs too!

Sanjay told me that, so far, he'd been on the merry-go-round and the octopus. Plus he'd nearly won a teddy on the claw of destiny.

When I asked him what a claw of destiny was, he said it was a really exciting game in a glass box where

you have to try and pick up a teddy by steering and dropping down a shiny metal claw.

Sanjay's dad is a crane driver so Sanjay

knew he would be really good at the claw of destiny. Trouble is, the claw dropped into the teddies before it was supposed to and then it closed up before it was supposed to as well. Which meant that Sanjay touched a teddy but didn't actually pick it up. But he was really close!

When I asked him what an octopus did, he said it was a really scary giant ride with eight legs that spins you round and round in the air! Plus it waves you up and down so much it nearly throws you out of the fairground!

When I asked him if it made him

scream, he said he screamed so loud, his ears nearly fell off!

When we got to the front of the queue for the waltzer, Nanny asked Sanjay's mum and dad if they wanted to get in our carriage with us. Waltzer carriages are easily big enough to fit six people in, so now it was going to be six times as much fun!

Waltzers are really death-defying. In fact they are so death-defying you don't get normal seat belts to save you, you get safety bars made out of actual metal!

Which is a good job really because waltzers are out of control!! Not only do they make you go faster than a rocket, they move you up and down as well!

After about twenty-seven seconds, we were all screaming so much we didn't even realize there was a steering wheel we could turn in the middle of our carriage. But when we noticed someone else doing it, we worked out how to make our carriage spin round too!

At first, Sanjay and me took turns with the wheel, but then our face muscles started to hurt so much from all our laughing and screaming that we had to stop. Which was OK,

because then Sanjay's dad did the wheel-turning instead.

You should have seen Nanny and Grampy's faces as we got spinnier and spinnier! Grampy's wrinkles went right over to one side of his face! And Nanny screamed so much, her false teeth nearly came out of her mouth!

I think Nanny and Grampy were really relieved when the waltzer started to slow down. Sanjay and me weren't. We wanted to stay on and have another go!

But we weren't allowed to.

Which was OK, because as the safety bars in our waltzer unlocked,

I saw another funfair game that I absolutely totally wanted to go on.

It was a Wild West game called rootin' tootin' shoot 'em. And guess what? It was a game with actual guns!

CHAPTER 12

The **trouble with actual guns** is Sanjay's mum and dad don't think children should be allowed to play with them.

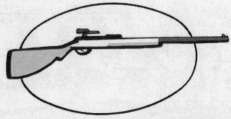

So we had to say goodbye to Sanjay and his mum and dad after that. Which was OK, because six people aren't allowed to hold a rootin' tootin' cowboy rifle at the same time.

Rootin' tootin' shoot 'em is one of the most dangerous things you can do at a funfair, because – and you're never going to believe this – it's a game with real actual rifles, loaded with real actual corks!

Once Grampy had paid a man in a cowboy hat some money, I was given five actual corks to shoot, all of my very own!!! Plus I was allowed to stand up on a box so I could reach my gun!

That's when I got to see what Grampy and me had to aim at. That's when I realized what a good shot I was going to have to be.

Because our targets weren't Indians or buffaloes.

They were boxes of dolly mixtures.

The **trouble with dolly mixtures** is they're a lot smaller than Indians and buffaloes. Which makes them a lot harder to aim at. And hit.

Grampy said to pretend I was Jesse James, but I don't think pop stars know anything about shooting dolly mixtures.

So I just decided to aim as best I could.

The **trouble with rootin' tootin' rifles** is they are quite heavy, which makes them hard to lift.

The **trouble with rootin' tootin' corks** is they don't know how to aim properly.

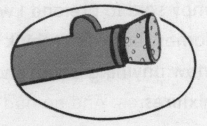

EVERY time the man in the cowboy hat loaded a cork for me, it came out of my rifle the wrong way when I shot it.

If I aimed a cork at the middle of the dolly mixtures, it went *over* the dolly mixtures.

If I aimed my cork over the dolly mixtures, it went *under* the dolly mixtures.

If I pointed my cork to the left, it went to the right.

And if I pointed my cork to the right, it went to the left!

Even Grampy couldn't hit a box of dolly mixtures. And he had five

corks too! Plus he was a soldier in
the war! At least I think he was.

On my last cork, I didn't even aim
at the dolly mixtures. I just pointed it
in the air and pulled the trigger.

And guess what?

I HIT THE DOLLY MIXTURES! I
knocked an actual box of actual
dolly mixtures right over with my
actual cork!

Trouble is, although I had
knocked the dolly mixtures over,
I hadn't knocked them OFF the
shelf.

Which means the man in the cowboy hat told me I hadn't won a prize.

Which wasn't OK. Because now I was starting to get a bit cross.

CHAPTER 13

The **trouble with getting a bit cross at a funfair** is it makes you need a really big lolly with coloured swirls on it.

Which is lucky really, because guess what I saw when we left the rootin' tootin' shoot 'em stall? Another stall that sold really big lollies with coloured swirls on them!

Nanny said that lollies with coloured swirls on them were better than dolly mixtures any day, and after about six licks I decided she was right.

After about fourteen

licks I decided I was going to try even harder to win a prize at the funfair. Then, about three licks later, I remembered exactly what prize I was going to win first.

A goldfish!!!!!!

The **trouble with going to win a goldfish** is you need to know where to go.

Grampy said he had been keeping an eye out for a stall where I could win a goldfish, but he hadn't seen one anywhere.

I tried looking with two eyes and I couldn't see anywhere either.

Nanny said that when she was my age, just about every stall at the funfair gave you a goldfish in a bag as a prize. Which sounded a bit odd at first, but then Grampy told me the bag was made of plastic and filled with water so the fish could breathe. Which meant that if you won a goldfish in a bag at a funfair, you could take it home and turn it into a pet!

Which made me want to win one even more!

Trouble is, there weren't any

goldfish that I could win.

There were loads of other prizes like teddies with wonky eyes, packs of cards with dragons on, squishy balls, bucket-and-spade sets in springy bags, little plastic guitars and blow-up bananas. But no alive goldfish in filled-up plastic bags.

When Grampy asked a stallholder where all the goldfish were, the stallholder told us that goldfish prizes had been banned from funfairs years

ago. Apparently olden days children used to win goldfish, take them home, but not look after them properly.

Which I can believe actually, because I had a pet goldfish of my own once called Freddy and my mum didn't look after him properly either. She let his water go all green.

Mum said the water was my responsibility, but there was no way that it was. I only said I would look after Freddy. I never EVER said I would look after his water.

In the end Mum gave Freddy to our neighbour, Mrs Pike, to look after, because she had a pond in her garden with nice clean water in it.

Which is a good job really, because if my mum had been left in charge of Freddy, I reckon she would have been arrested by the RSPCA. She might even have gone to prison for goldfish neglect.

The **trouble with Mum going to prison for goldfish neglect** is she wouldn't be able to make my tea.

Or take me to school. Or read me bedtime stories.

So it's probably a good job we couldn't win a goldfish at the funfair.

And anyway, you'll never guess what I suddenly saw next!

Actual POPCORN! I'd never had actual popcorn before!

The **trouble with actual popcorn** is there are two different flavours. Normal and toffee.

The **trouble with normal and toffee** is I like them both the same.

Nanny thought I might have been full after my slush puppy, hotdog, burger, tomato sauce, candyfloss and swirly lolly, but I told her I definitely wasn't.

So she let me have a big box of each!

Trouble is, then I saw the helter-skelter!

The **trouble with helter-skelters** is you're not allowed to go down them with a box of popcorn in each hand.

 I know because when I got to the top of the stairs, the helter-skelter man made me go all the way back down. Which was a bit tricky because there were loads of children coming up the other way.

Nanny and Grampy said they would hold my popcorn for me and meet me at the bottom of the slide. Which was handy really because you need both your hands to go down a helter-skelter slide. One for holding onto your sack, and the other one for waving.

Helter-skelters are one of the highest things you can do at a funfair. When you get to the top of the slide, you can see all the rides and stalls down below you, from one corner of the funfair right over to the other! And you can see all the people who are going bald!

Before you go down the helter-skelter slide, you have to put your legs and bottom inside a sack. Then the helter-skelter man gives you a push, and off you go!

I'd never been on a slide as whizzy as a helter-skelter slide before. Or a slide that was so curly and

bendy! When I got to the bottom I thought I was going to shoot right off the end, but luckily my sack knew when to stop.

Nanny and Grampy asked me if I wanted to go on again, and I nearly did, but then I noticed the hoopla!

The **trouble with the hoopla** is it's one of the hardest throwing games in the world.

It looks easy, but when you try it, it actually ends up being really hard.

The way you play hoopla is you give a lady some money, and then she gives you three hoops. Then you have to aim your hoops at some twenty-pound notes that are elastic-banded to some boxes. Real actual twenty-pound notes that you can actually win!

At first I thought you had to throw your hoops over the money to win. But then Nanny told me that my hoop had to go over the money AND the box underneath it as well.

Not just any old over. EXACTLY over.

The **trouble with hoopla hoops** is they have round sides and the boxes have square sides. Which meant my hoops wouldn't fit over the boxes.

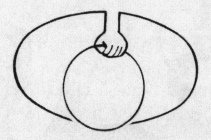

When I asked the hoopla lady for some square hoops, she said she didn't have any. Which meant I couldn't win with my first hoop. I couldn't win with my second hoop.

And I couldn't win with my third hoop either. And neither could Nanny or Grampy.

Which made me
feel really, really
cross.

Grampy said he'd
never won at hoopla in his entire life.
Which makes you think, doesn't it? If
people can't win at the games, why
do the funfair people keep on doing
them?

After the hoopla, I was absolutely
determined to win a prize. In fact I
was so determined and so cross, I
decided I wasn't going to go on any
other rides AT ALL, UNTIL I HAD WON
AN ACTUAL PRIZE ON AN ACTUAL
GAME AT THE FUNFAIR!

I wouldn't even go on the octopus until I'd won a prize!

I'm telling you, I was SOOOOO determined . . .

And I was SOOOOOOOOOOOOOOO cross . . .

It made me need an ice cream.

CHAPTER 14

The **trouble with funfair ice creams** is you have to pay more if you want flumps on them.

And you have to pay even more if you want strawberry sauce as well.

Marshmallow flumps are one of my favourite ice-cream sprinkles, and strawberry sauce is one of my

top squirty things in the world. So once
Grampy had given the ice-cream lady
some money, I absolutely
had to have both.

And a flake.

Nanny thought I
must definitely be full

after my slush puppy, hotdog, burger, tomato sauce, candyfloss, swirly lolly and two boxes of popcorn. But the good thing about popcorn is it's really light. So it means you'll always have room for ice cream, flumps, strawberry sauce and a chocolate flake.

Especially on a really hot day.

The **trouble with eating funfair ice creams on really hot days** is you have to eat them really, really quickly.

Otherwise your ice cream will melt, which means your flumps might fall off and your flake might come out. Plus your strawberry sauce might dribble down your cornet and go all over your hand.

Luckily I'm an expert at eating ice creams really, really fast. Which is handy, because if I'd eaten my ice cream any slower, I would absolutely, totally never have been ready to go on . . .

. . . wait for it . . .

Have you guessed it . . . ?

THE COCONUT SHY!!!!!!!

When Grampy told me he'd seen

an actual coconut shy at the funfair, I nearly dropped my last bit of cornet!

A coconut shy isn't a shy coconut, by the way – it's a game where you get to throw really hard balls.

At first I couldn't see the coconut shy anywhere because there were too many people. Luckily Grampy is taller than me so it was easy for him to point the way.

The **trouble with pointing the way** is it still doesn't stop a funfair from being really crowded.

But once we'd squeezed past a really, really long queue for the roller coaster and a much shorter queue for a ride called the teacups, I saw the coconut shy with my very own eyes. Plus I saw the actual coconuts that Grampy said we were going to win! They were sitting on the top of some long sticks that the coconut-shy man had banged into the grass.

At the front, lots of people were lined up, throwing balls at the back of the tent. Every time they hit the back of the tent, the balls dropped down and landed on the grass.

"I can do that! I know I can do that!" I said to Grampy. "All I need is some balls!"

Once Grampy had paid the coconut-shy man some money, I was given five balls of my very own! They were quite small balls, but they were made of hard, roundish wood, which meant they went a really long way when you threw them.

After I'd thrown all five of my balls, I was absolutely sure I'd won a prize, because every single one of my balls hit the back of the tent and every

160

single one of them rolled down and fell onto the grass!

Just like everybody else's!

Trouble is, that isn't what you have to do to win a coconut. I thought it was, because that's what everyone else was doing.

To win a coconut at a coconut shy, you actually have to knock an actual coconut off an actual stick.

Which means you have to aim at the actual coconuts with your balls.

Grampy said that was what everyone throwing the balls was trying to do. But it didn't look like it to me. Some people weren't even getting close!

Now that I knew the rules of how to play, Nanny said I should have another go. So I did.

Trouble is, I missed all five times again.

The **trouble with missing all five times again** is it makes you start to get cross again.

And it makes you need another go.

Once Nanny had given the man some more money, Grampy stood behind me and told me how to aim. He told me to put one foot forward and one foot back, point at the coconut with my free hand, hold my wooden ball as far back as I could with my throwing hand, close one eye and BLAM IT!

So I did.

But I missed again.

Which made eleven balls I hadn't hit a coconut with. Which made me feel even crosser.

So I aimed again.

The **trouble with aiming at a coconut when you're cross** is it makes your eyes go googly, which means you miss by even more.

Especially if when you let go of the ball, you growl as well.

When Grampy heard me growl, I think he got a bit nervous, so he asked the coconut-shy man if I could stand a bit nearer on my next throw. Which is totally fair because, if you ask me, the more balls you buy, the nearer to the coconuts you should be able to get.

When the coconut-shy man said I could step in front of the line to do my next throw, I was sure I would be able to hit a coconut.

Except I didn't.

I missed again. Or at least my ball did.

Which made me the crossest I'd been all day. And the growliest.

So Grampy asked if I could stand a bit nearer still.

The **trouble with standing a bit nearer still** is the coconut-shy man said I was standing too close now. Which I wasn't.

But he said I was. So I had to step back a bit.

Which put me off.

Which meant that I missed with my fourteenth ball as well.

And my fifteenth.

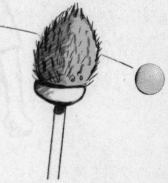

Because I was still feeling a bit put off.

Which made me want to punch all the coconuts and kick all the sticks over. And scream louder than any scream I'd done all day.

But I didn't. Because Grampy said he'd win me a coconut instead.

CHAPTER 15

Once Grampy had paid the coconut-shy man some more money I was sure he'd win me a coconut. But on his first throw he only hit the back of the tent. Grampy said he was just getting his eye in with his first shot, and that he was sure that he would hit a coconut with his second throw.

Trouble is, he didn't. His second ball went

right over the top of the coconuts.

Grampy said that the second ball had slipped out of his hand by mistake and that his third ball had coconut written all over it. (But I don't know who by.)

Then he told us to watch and learn.

The **trouble with watching and learning** is sometimes you're not sure what to watch and learn.

Because not only did Grampy

miss again, he pulled a muscle in his shoulder.

Nanny said it served him right for throwing the ball so hard. Trouble is, now that his shoulder was pulled, Grampy had to retire injured with two balls left to throw!

The **trouble with having two balls left to throw** is you then have to decide who is going to throw them.

I thought I should probably have the last two goes, because I had the most coconut-ball-throwing experience. But then Nanny said, "Why don't we throw one each?"

Which actually was a really good idea, because guess what? You're never going to believe this . . .

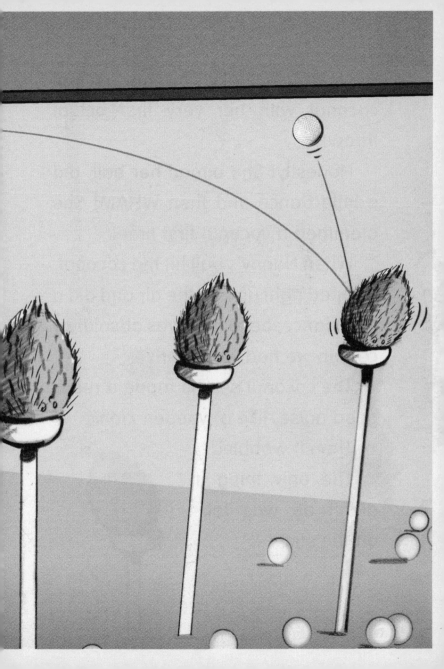

Nanny actually hit an actual coconut with her very first actual throw!!!

Honestly! She aimed her ball, did a little dance and then WHAM! She blammed a coconut first time!

When Nanny's ball hit the coconut, I leaped right up into the air and did a little dance, because I was absolutely certain we had won a prize.

The coconut she hit made a really good noise, like a wooden *clonk*.

Then it wobbled.

The only thing it didn't do was fall off the stick.

Instead of falling off, it just stayed there!

Grampy said Nanny should have thrown her ball harder, but Nanny said if she had, she would have pulled her shoulder too.

I said if you hit a coconut you should win the coconut. Trouble is, the coconut-shy man wouldn't change the rules.

Which made me crosser and more furious than I've ever been in my whole life!

Which is why I threw the last ball at him.

The **trouble with throwing a wooden ball at a coconut-shy man** is if it hits him on the head it could kill him.

Luckily I only hit him on the leg.

Actually, it wasn't even his leg. It was only his knee.

I know it was his knee because it sounded like a coconut.

Nanny and Grampy said they were really disappointed in me

when I threw my last ball at the coconut-shy man. In fact they were so disappointed in me that they made me say sorry.

But guess what? Even though I said sorry, the coconut-shy man STILL banned me from having any more goes. Or from coming within ten metres of his stall.

Which meant now I was NEVER going to win a coconut at the funfair! EVER!

And all because I'd hit a great big coconut-shy man on the leg with a teensy wooden ball!

CHAPTER 16

The **trouble with realizing you're NEVER going to be able to win a coconut EVER in your WHOLE LIFE** is it makes you growl even louder.

Nanny said only grizzly bears were meant to do the kind of growls I was doing and that perhaps it would be better if I sat down on the grass for a

while to calm down.

The **trouble with sitting down on the grass** is it makes me want a toffee apple.

Grampy said there were plenty more prizes we could still win at the fair, but if a toffee apple would stop me growling, it would probably be a good idea.

A toffee apple is an apple dipped in really hard toffee. The toffee is really reddish and you have to bite right through it to get to the juicy apple bit inside.

Nanny said she was amazed I still had room in my tummy for anything, after my slush puppy, hotdog, burger, tomato sauce, candyfloss, swirly lolly, two boxes of popcorn, ice cream, flumps, strawberry sauce and chocolate flake. But toffee apples aren't that filling at all. Because the biggest bit of a toffee apple is made of actual fruit. Plus some of it you can't even eat, like the apple core in the middle or the stick.

Grampy said that once I'd finished nibbling my toffee apple stick we should decide which prize we were going to try and win next. But just as I was putting my toffee apple stick in the bin, we bumped into Mrs Peters!

Mrs Peters said if I kept trying my hardest she was absolutely sure I would win a prize at one of the funfair games soon.

And you'd think she should know, wouldn't you, because she's my teacher.

Trouble is, she was wrong.

The **trouble with the clown bonk** was the clowns kept disappearing before I could bonk them.

The **trouble with the test-your-strength stall** was the hammer was too heavy for me to lift.

The **trouble with hot-shot basketball** was the hoop was too high for me to get the balls in.

The **trouble with tin can alley** was the beanbags I was aiming with went floppy every time I threw them.

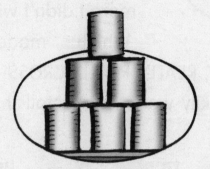

And **the trouble with roll-a-penny** was my pennies wouldn't roll straight at all.

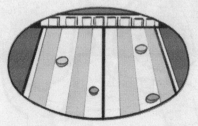

It was hopeless! The harder and harder I tried, the more and more I didn't win!

Which made me REALLY, REALLY, REALLY CROSS!

Luckily we found a stall that sold fudge.

The brilliant thing about fudge is it comes in loads of different square-shaped flavours.

At first I thought I was only allowed one type of flavour fudge in my bag, but the lady in front of us in the queue got three types put in hers.

So I decided to have six flavours: caramel, vanilla, coconut ice, raspberry ripple, chocolate and mint. I was going to have rum and raisin too, but I decided not to in the end, because rum and raisin sounds like it's got beer in it.

Plus I didn't want to be greedy.

Grampy said I should think of

every piece of fudge in my bag as a well-earned prize for trying so hard to win something!

Which made me feel a lot better.

Because when I looked in my bag I still had eight prizes left!

While I was eating a mint one, I thought about ALL the other lovely things that Nanny and Grampy had bought me at the funfair that day – the slush puppy, hotdog, burger, tomato sauce, candyfloss, swirly lolly, two boxes of popcorn, ice cream, flumps, strawberry sauce, chocolate flake and toffee apple. Then I realized that all those were just like prizes too! And I hadn't even had to win them! Nanny and Grampy had just given them to me! That's when I realized what a lucky person I was!

By the time I'd eaten all my squares of fudge, I didn't care about winning actual prizes any more at all! I just decided I was going to have as much fun at the funfair with Nanny and Grampy as I possibly could before it was time to go home.

And boy did we have fun!

First, we went on the big dipper.

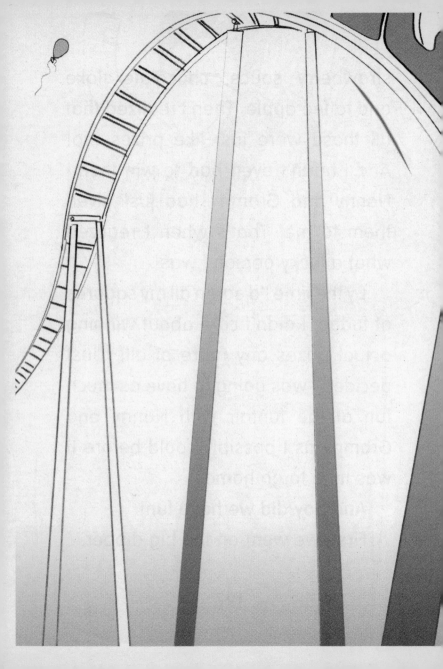

Big dippers are the dippiest things you can do at a funfair.

Then we went on the pirate galleon.

Pirate galleons are the scariest things you can do a funfair. I even saw Dylan doing massive screams!

Then we went in the hall of mirrors!
Halls of mirrors are the funniest-
looking things you can do at a funfair.

Then we went on the octopus! And believe me, Sanjay Lapore was right!

All the rides at the funfair were soooooo much fun! Not just for me, but for all my school friends too!!

I saw Fiona Tucker waving to me on the merry-go-round.

I saw David Alexander pretending to aim at me with the water squirters.

Stephanie Brakespeare got so dizzy on the vortex, she had to go and sit inside an actual St John's ambulance till she felt right again.

Nanny and Grampy said that they wouldn't mind a sit-down too. Not in an ambulance – on a bench.

The **trouble with benches** is they aren't very exciting.

They don't zoom up or down or spin round and round or anything. They ARE free, but after about two seconds, they get really boring.

So Nanny and Grampy said I could go for a little walk by myself. As long as I stayed where they could see me.

That's when I met Jasmine Smart, Nishta Bagwhat, Colin Kettle, Barry Morely, Barry Morely's big brother and two of his friends.

That's when everything started to go a bit wrong.

CHAPTER 17

The **trouble with Jasmine Smart, Nishta Bagwhat, Colin Kettle, Barry Morely, Barry Morely's big brother and two of his friends** is they had all been to the funfair the night before.

And none of them had won on the coconuts either.

Nishta had had ten goes and missed every time.

Jasmine had had five goes and got really close.

Colin and Barry had had twenty goes each! Plus Barry had hit the same coconut two times in a row and both times the coconut hadn't fallen off!

When I told them that the same thing had happened to me, Grampy and Nanny, no one was in the slightest bit surprised.

Because do you know what Barry's big brother had told them?

He'd told Barry, Nishta, Jasmine and Colin that the coconuts in the coconut shy at the funfair will never EVER fall off! Because they are stuck on with super-strength coconut glue!!!!!

And do you know what Barry's big brother's friends had told them as well?

They had told them that the coconuts at the funfair aren't just glued on – there are invisible force fields around all of them too!!

I'd only ever seen invisible force fields in space films before. I never knew you could get them around coconuts. But according to Barry's big brother's

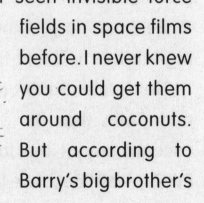

friends, the coconut-shy man had a secret force-field gadget in his trouser pocket. Which meant every time he saw you do a good throw he would make you miss by clicking the button and turning a force field on around the coconut you had aimed at!!!

Colin Kettle said that knocking off a glued-on coconut would be a really hard thing to do. And Nishta said knocking off a glued-on coconut with a force field around it would be totally impossible.

Which made me get really cross all over again.

In fact, it made me get so cross, I wanted to scream and growl and stamp my feet all at the same time!!!

Which is why I said I would help Barry, Colin, Nishta and Jasmine tell everyone at the whole funfair what a swizz coconut shies are.

Which is why I said I would join them in a really big coconut-shy protest.

Which is why I said I would meet them at the big wheel at four o'clock.

Which wasn't my fault.

CHAPTER 18

The **trouble with doing a protest** is you're not really sure what a protest is going to be until you've actually done one.

Barry said that his big brother had come up with a really good plan for a protest and that he and his friends were going to give us all the things we needed to make it the best funfair protest ever!

All I had to do was be by the big wheel at four o'clock.

The **trouble with being by the big wheel at four o'clock** is I was meant to be home by four o'clock.

Which meant I had to persuade Nanny and Grampy to stay a little longer. When Nanny looked at her watch and saw it was quarter to four, she said that we really ought to be heading back to the car. But when I told her that the big wheel was the only ride I hadn't had a chance to go on, Grampy persuaded her to stay!

Nanny and Grampy said that they were feeling a bit tired and they would find another bench to sit on and wave to me as I went round. Which was good really, because I wasn't sure if they would want to join in our coconut-shy protest.

When I got to the big wheel, Barry's big brother and his friends were sitting on the grass smiling. Nishta, Jasmine, Colin and Barry were all waiting for me at the end of the queue.

When I joined up with them, we all did a high-five together and then Nishta gave me a big piece of paper to hide under my T-shirt.

Barry told me it was my secret protest poster, but I wasn't allowed to take it out until I got the secret signal.

Then Colin gave me something even more exciting. A tube of superglue!

"We've all got superglue. And we've all got posters," whispered Nishta.

Then they told me the plan.

The **trouble with plans** is they sound really good until they go wrong.

The first bit of our plan went really well, because all we had to do was pay the big-wheel man some money and wait for him to let us on.

The third bit of our plan went really well too.

It was the second bit that got us into trouble.

As soon as the big wheel started to turn, Nishta pulled her poster out from under her T-shirt and held it above her head just like she said she would.

"I'm a coconut!" she shouted at the very top of her voice.

Which was the secret signal for Barry.

"I'm a coconut!" he shouted, holding up his poster too.

Which was the secret signal for Jasmine. And then Colin and then me.

By the time all five of us had shouted, "I'm a coconut!" we were right at the top of the big wheel! Which meant everyone in the funfair could see us! And hear us!

Every time the big wheel went back down to the bottom, I waved as hard as I could to Nanny and Grampy. And every time the big wheel went back to the top, I shouted, "I'm a coconut!" as loud as I could to everyone down below!

It was brilliant!

Until the big wheel came to a stop.

The **trouble with big wheels stopping** is everybody expects you to get off. Especially the big-wheel man waiting at the bottom.

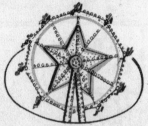

Trouble is, getting off wasn't part of our plan.

Staying on was.

When the big-wheel man asked Nishta to get out of her seat, she shook her head and held her protest poster high up above her head.

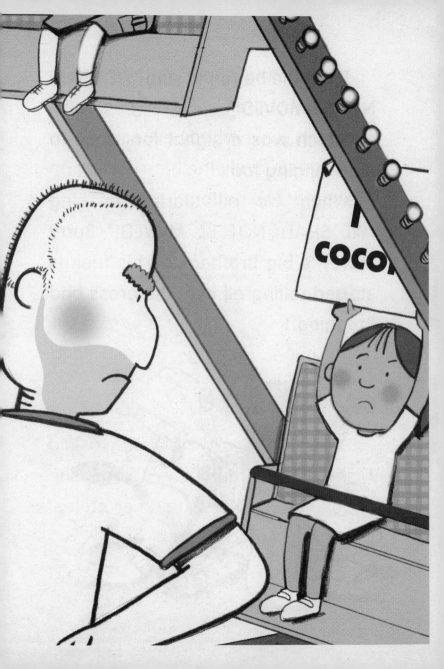

Then she began to sing "WE SHALL NOT BE MOVED!"

Which was a signal for us all to start singing too.

When we all started to sing "WE SHALL NOT BE MOVED!" Barry Morely's big brother and his friends started rolling all over the grass and laughing.

The big-wheel man didn't laugh, though. He got cross instead. Mostly I think because he had a long line of people queuing and he couldn't let them on unless we moved.

"Off the wheel NOW!" he said to Nishta. "I've got people waiting to get on!"

That's when Nishta told him that we had glued ourselves to our seats.

The **trouble with telling a big-wheel man that you've glued yourself to your seat** is at first he doesn't believe you.

Especially if it's five seats.

Even nannies and grampies don't believe you.

But when you show them your empty superglue tubes and try to stand up, they change their mind.

Then they call the fire brigade.

The **trouble with calling the fire brigade** is it takes quite a long time for them to arrive.

Which meant I was going to be even later getting home now. Which meant Nanny and Grampy had to call my mum and tell her what I'd done as well.

When the firemen arrived at the funfair and found out that we were coconuts glued to our seats, they told Nanny that they were going to

have to cut a hole in my new orange shorts.

And my pants.

Which was a bit embarrassing really. Especially for Colin, because he didn't have any pants on.

It took the firemen about two hours to cut Nishta, Barry, Jasmine, Colin and me out of our seats. And after that, the big wheel had to be closed for repairs. Which made the big-wheel man go the same colour as my slush puppy.

When he threatened to sue Nishta's mum and dad for loss of earnings, Nanny and Grampy went a bit of a funny colour too. Then they suggested we walk back to the car as quickly as we could.

On the way, Grampy told me

that we had been tricked into doing something very silly by Barry Morely's big brother and his big-boy friends. That's why they were rolling all over the grass and laughing at us so much as we went round and round on the big wheel.

Which made me start growling all over again.

Nanny said that big boys can be really immature sometimes and that from now on it might be better if me and my friends ignored anything we ever heard big boys say. Especially big-boy talk about coconuts, glue and invisible force fields.

When we got near to the coconut shy, I realized that Nanny and Grampy were right.

Because just as we walked past, I saw an actual coconut being knocked off an actual stick by an actual wooden ball.

When the boy who had thrown the ball turned round, put his shirt over his head and started running around like a footballer who had scored a goal, I nearly screamed!

Because do you know who it was?!

Do you know who had won an actual coconut at the funfair, with one really good throw?

It was JACK BEECHWHISTLE!

Of all the boys in all the funfair, it had to be HIM!

I was growling like a grizzly bear crossed with a dinosaur by the time I got back to the car.

CHAPTER 19

I didn't get home till twenty to seven this evening. Which isn't my bedtime, but for some unknown reason Mum has decided it is.

Nanny and Grampy said they were pleased that I'd had such a lovely time, but it might be a while before they took me to a funfair again.

Mum said that gluing myself to a piece of funfair equipment was an extremely silly thing to do and that ruining my new orange shorts was disgraceful. She said the hole in my

shorts was so big, she would have to throw them away. Which if you ask me, means she is just too lazy to sew them up.

Anyway, as a punishment, she said I would be going to bed without any grilled chicken, wild rice and broccoli for supper.

Which is OK actually. Because, to be honest, I am still a bit full from my slush puppy, hotdog, burger, tomato sauce, candyfloss, swirly lolly, two boxes of popcorn, ice cream, flumps, strawberry sauce,

chocolate flake,
toffee apple, and
mint, vanilla, coconut
ice, raspberry ripple,
chocolate and
caramel fudges.

Oh, and two
of Nanny's mints. (I had
another one on the way
home!)

Tee-hee!

P.S. I bet you thought
I was going to be sick!

DAISY'S TROUBLE INDEX

The trouble with . . .

Have you read Daisy's other stories?

WHAT WILL DAISY DO NEXT?!

Accidentally on Purpose

A split-page book with ninety naughty nix-ups!

Kes Gray & Nick Sharratt

006 and a Bit

Kes Gray & Nick Sharratt

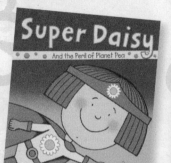

Super Daisy

And the Peril of Planet Pea

Kes Gray & Nick Sharratt

Yuk!

Kes Gray & Nick Sharratt

You Do!

Kes Gray & Nick Sharratt

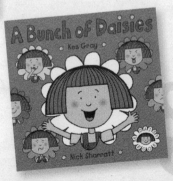

A Bunch of Daisies

Kes Gray

Nick Sharratt

DAISY
and the TROUBLE with
LIFE

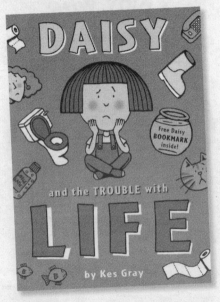

It's SOOOOOOOOOOOOOOO unfair.
Daisy's been grounded. No HOPPING or SKIPPING, FLYING or PARACHUTING.
She's lucky she's even been allowed out of her bedroom after what she's done.
But what HAS she done that is SOOOOOOOOOOOOOO naughty?

DAISY
and the TROUBLE with
GIANTS

Fee Fi Fo Fum, NOW what's Daisy done?!
Daisy has decided she wants to meet a REAL GIANT! But REALLY BIG
TROUBLE looms as she hunts high and low for a magic bean!

DAISY

and the TROUBLE with

ZOOS

Daisy loves surprises! Especially special birthday surprises – like a trip to the ZOO!!! Who'd have guessed a rhino could do so much wee all in one go! Who'd have imagined an elephant tooth was that heavy! TROUBLE is, the biggest surprise is yet to come.

DAISY
and the TROUBLE with
KITTENS

Daisy is going on holiday! In an actual plane to actual Spain!
It's so exciting! She's never seen a palm tree before, or eaten octopus,
or played Zombie Mermaids, or made so many new friends!
TROUBLE is, five of them are small and cute and furry!

DAISY
and the TROUBLE with
CHRISTMAS

It's Christmas and Daisy has been given an actual part in the actual school Christmas play! She has special lines to learn and even a special costume to wear!! Trouble is . . . there's something about baby Jesus that isn't quite special enough . . .

www.daisyclub.co.uk

DAISY
and the TROUBLE with
MAGGOTS

Look out, ducks! Look out, canoeists! Daisy is going fishing for the very
first time! She's got an actual fishing rod that catches actual
fish, an actual bait box full of actual maggots, PLUS an actual
fishing catapult that pings, twangs and BLAMS . . . oh dear.